For Stefanie

DIAL BOOKS FOR YOUNG READERS
A division of Penguin Young Readers Group
Published by the Penguin Group
Penguin Group (USA) Inc., 375 Hudson Street, New York, New York 10014, USA

USA / Canada / UK / Ireland / Australia / New Zealand / India / South Africa / China
Penguin Books Ltd, Registered Offices: 80 Strand, London WC2R 0RL, England
For more information about the Penguin Group visit penguin.com

Text and illustrations copyright © 2013 by Stephen Savage

Library of Congress Cataloging-in-Publication Data
Savage, Stephen, date, author, illustrator.
 Ten orange pumpkins / by Stephen Savage.
    pages cm
 Summary: "In this Halloween countdown book, ten orange pumpkins are
each carried off by a witch, a ghost, a spider, and other Halloween
creatures until there's just one" —Provided by publisher.
 ISBN 978-0-8037-3938-3 (hardcover)
 [1. Stories in rhyme. 2. Pumpkin—Fiction. 3. Jack-o-lanterns—Fiction.
4. Halloween—Fiction. 5. Counting.] I. Title.
 PZ8.3.S2454Te 2013
 [E]—dc23   2012042091

Manufactured in China on acid-free paper • 10 9 8 7 6 5 4 3 2 1

Designed by Stephen Savage and Lily Malcom • Text set in Agilita Bold
The publisher does not have any control over and does not assume any responsibility for author or third-party websites or their content.

The artwork for this book was created using digital and traditional media. No pumpkins were harmed in the making of this book.

Thanks to Brenda, Robin, and Wes.

TEN ORANGE PUMPKINS

A COUNTING BOOK BY STEPHEN SAVAGE

Dial Books for Young Readers   An imprint of Penguin Group (USA) Inc.

Ten orange pumpkins,
fresh off the vine.
Tonight will be a spooky night.

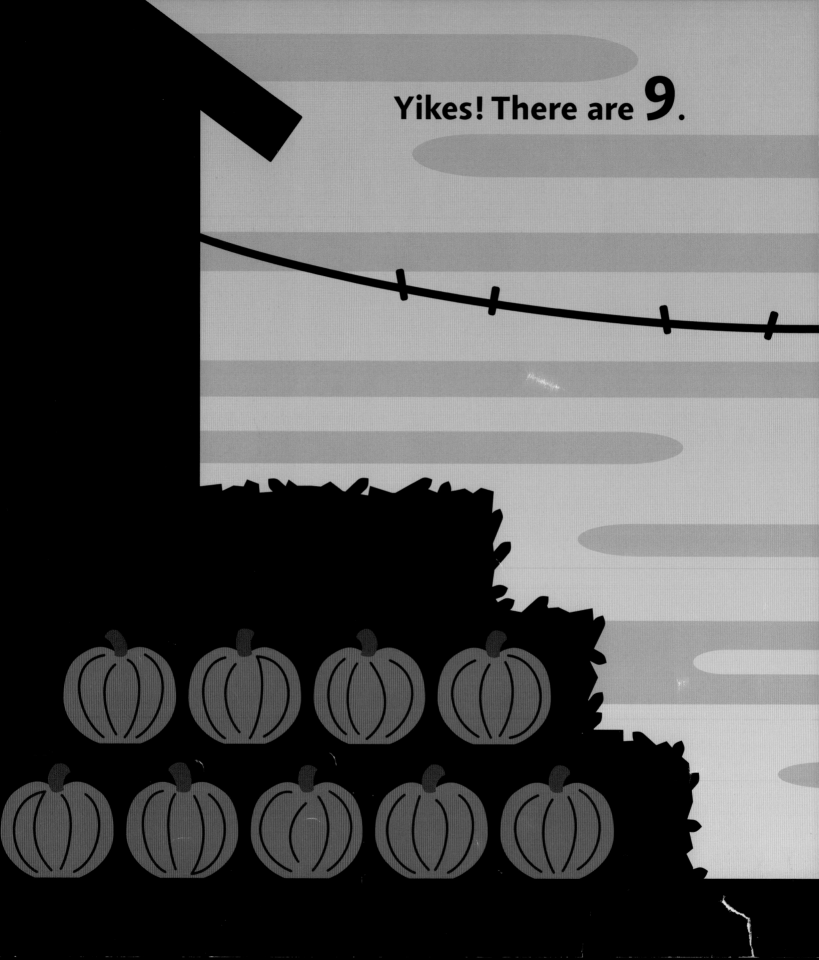

Yikes! There are 9.

Nine orange pumpkins
sit outside the gate.
Which one will the mummy choose?

Hah! There are 8.

Eight orange pumpkins
Beneath a starry heaven.
Thunderclouds come rolling in.

Flash! There are **7**.

Seven orange pumpkins
ripe for treats and tricks.
Something sweet is in the air.

Boo! There are **6.**

Six orange pumpkins
out for a drive.
Watch out! There's a bump ahead.

Splash! There are **5**.

Four orange pumpkins
by an old oak tree.
Owl swoops down on
silent wings.

Whoosh! There are **3**.

Three orange pumpkins.
A pot of witches' brew.
This will add a tasty touch!

Poof! There are 2.

Two orange pumpkins.
A sticky web is spun.
Look who's crawling closer now.

Gasp! There's only 1.

One orange pumpkin
nowhere to be seen.

Here it is,
all aglow.

Happy
Halloween!